The Smartest GIANT in Town

Written by Julia Donaldson

Illustrated by Axel Scheffler

MACMILLAN CHILDREN'S BOOKS

George was a giant, the scruffiest giant in town.
He always wore the same pair of old brown sandals
and the same old patched-up gown.

"I wish I wasn't the scruffiest giant in town,"
he said sadly.

But one day, George noticed a new shop.

It was full of smart clothes. So he bought . . .

a smart shirt,

a smart pair of trousers,

a smart belt,

a smart stripy tie,

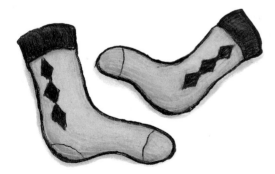

some smart socks
with diamonds up the sides,

and a pair of
smart shiny shoes.

"Now I'm the smartest giant in town," he said proudly.

George left his old clothes
behind in the shop.
He was about to go home
when he heard a sound.

On the pavement stood a giraffe who was sniffing sadly.
"What's the matter?" asked George.

"It's my neck," said the giraffe. "It's so very long and so very cold. I wish I had a long, warm scarf!"

"Cheer up!" said George, and he took off his stripy tie.
"It didn't match my socks anyway," he said, as he
wound it round and round the giraffe's neck.
It made a wonderful scarf.
"Thank you!" said the giraffe.

As George strode towards home, he sang to himself,

"My tie is a scarf for a cold giraffe,

But look me up and down –

I'm the smartest giant in town."

George came to a river. On a boat stood a goat who was bleating loudly. "What's the matter?" asked George.

"It's my sail," said the goat.

"It blew away in a storm.

"I wish I had a strong new sail
for my boat!"

"Cheer up!" said George, and he took off his new white shirt. "It kept coming untucked anyway," he said, as he tied it to the mast of the goat's boat. It made a magnificent sail.

"Thank you!" said the goat.

George strode on, singing to himself,

"My tie is a scarf for a cold giraffe,

My shirt's on a boat as a sail for a goat,

But look me up and down –

I'm the smartest giant in town!"

George came to a tiny ruined house.
Beside the house stood a white mouse with
lots of baby mice. They were all squeaking.
"What's the matter?" asked George.

"It's our house,"
squeaked the mother mouse.

"It burned down, and now
we have nowhere to live.

"I wish we had
a nice new house!"

"Cheer up!" said George, and he took off one of his shiny shoes. "It was giving me blisters anyway," he said, as the mouse and her babies scrambled inside. The shoe made a perfect home for them.

"Thank you!" they squeaked.

George had to hop along the road now, but he didn't mind. As he hopped, he sang to himself,

"My tie is a scarf for a cold giraffe,

My shirt's on a boat as a sail for a goat,

My shoe is a house for a little white mouse,

But look me up and down –

I'm the smartest giant in town."

George came to a campsite.
Beside a tent stood a fox
who was crying.
"What's the matter?"
asked George.

"It's my sleeping bag,"
said the fox.

"I dropped it in a puddle.

"I wish I had a warm, dry sleeping bag!"

"Cheer up!" said George, and he took off one of his socks with diamonds up the sides. "It was tickling my toes anyway," he said, as the fox snuggled into it. It made a very fine sleeping bag.

"Thank you!" said the fox.

George hopped on, singing to himself,

"My tie is a scarf for a cold giraffe,
    My shirt's on a boat as a sail for a goat,
    My shoe is a house for a little white mouse,
    One of my socks is a bed for a fox,
      But look me up and down –
    I'm the smartest giant in town."

George came to a big squelchy bog.
Beside the bog stood a dog
who was howling.

"What's the matter?" asked George.

"It's this bog,"
said the dog.

"I need to get across, but I keep
getting stuck in the mud.

"I wish there was
a safe, dry path."

"Cheer up!" said George, and he took off his smart new belt. "It was squashing my tummy anyway," he said, as he laid it down over the bog. It made an excellent path.

"Thank you!" said the dog.

The wind started to blow, but George didn't mind.

He hopped on, singing to himself,

"My tie is a scarf for a cold giraffe,

My shirt's on a boat as a sail for a goat,

My shoe is a house for a little white mouse,

One of my socks is a bed for a fox,

My belt helped a dog who was crossing a bog,

But . . .

"My trousers are falling down!
I'm the coldest giant in town!"

Suddenly George felt sad and shivery and not at all smart.
He stood on one foot and thought. "I'll have to go back
to the shop and buy some more clothes," he decided.
   He turned round and hopped all the way back to the shop.

But when he got there, it was CLOSED!

"Oh, no!" cried George. He sank down onto the doorstep and a tear ran down his nose. He felt as sad as all the animals he had met on his way home.

Then, out of the corner of his eye, he saw a bag with something familiar poking out of the top. George took a closer look . . .

"My gown!" he yelled. "My dear old gown and sandals!" George put them on. They felt wonderfully comfortable.

"I'm the cosiest giant in town!" he cried, and he danced back home along the road.

Outside his front door stood all the animals he had helped.

They were carrying an enormous present.

"Come on, George," they said. "Open it!"

George untied the ribbon. Inside was a beautiful gold paper
crown and a card.

"Look inside the card, George!" said the animals.

George put the crown on his head and opened the card.

Inside, it said,

Your tie is a scarf
for a cold giraffe,
Your shirt's on a boat
as a sail for a goat,
Your shoe is a house
for a little white mouse,
One of your socks
is a bed for a fox,
Your belt helped a dog, who was
crossing a bog,
So here is a very
fine crown,
to go with the sandals and gown
of the KINDEST giant in
town.

For Lola – J.D.

First published 2002 by Macmillan Children's Books
First published in paperback 2003 by Macmillan Children's Books
This edition published 2011 for Bookstart by Macmillan Children's Books
a division of Macmillan Publishers Limited
20 New Wharf Road, London N1 9RR
Basingstoke and Oxford
Associated companies worldwide
www.panmacmillan.com

ISBN 978-1-4472-0705-4

Text copyright © Julia Donaldson 2002
Illustrations copyright © Axel Scheffler 2002
Moral rights asserted.

3 5 7 9 8 6 4 2

A CIP catalogue record for this book is available
from the British Library.

Printed in China